# The Curse of
# Rafferty McGill

# The Curse of Rafferty McGill

## Dianne M. MacMillan

Albert Whitman & Company
Morton Grove, Illinois

Library of Congress Cataloging-in-Publication Data

MacMillan, Dianne M., 1943-
The curse of Rafferty McGill / by Dianne M. MacMillan ;
illustrated by Guy Porfirio.
p. cm.
Summary: When a leprechaun grants Ryan O'Connor's wish one
St. Patrick's Day, Ryan must find a way to grant the leprechaun's
wish in return or his piano teacher, her house, and another
student will be gone forever.
ISBN 0-8075-3779-9 (hardcover)
[1. Leprechauns—Fiction. 2. Wishes—Fiction. 3. Magic—Fiction.
4. Shoes—Fiction. 5. Time management—Fiction.]
I. Porfirio, Guy, ill. II. Title.
PZ7.M2279Cu 2003 [Fic]—dc21 2003000238

The design is by Carol Gildar.

For more information about Albert Whitman & Company,
please visit our web site at www.albertwhitman.com.

*To Trevor and Madisen*

# Table of Contents

# Be Careful of Wishes

On St. Patrick's Day, Ryan O'Conner made his piano teacher disappear. The day started off like a normal Saturday. "Ryan," his mother called from the kitchen. "You're late for Miss Talbot's."

Ryan jumped up from the couch where he was watching television. "Move it, Benji. I gotta go!" He stepped over his little brother, who was sitting on the floor dressed in a leprechaun costume.

Mrs. O'Conner came into the room holding Ryan's piano music and jacket. "Did you sweep the garage?"

"Oh, I forgot. I'll do it later, Mom."

Benji got up from the floor. "Ryan, aren't you going to watch me in the St. Patrick's Day parade?"

"No, Benji. I've got piano lessons."

"But you can't leave now. You said you'd show

me that magic disappearing card trick."

"Benji, I'll show you later." Ryan grabbed his music and jacket from his mother and raced out the kitchen door.

Benji called out in a whiny voice, "You always say 'later.'"

Ryan put on his jacket. The air was chilly, and black clouds in the sky warned of rain. Looks like Benji isn't going to be in the parade, he thought. The wind pushed a tree branch back and forth against the side of his tree house. Ryan looked at his special hideout. For one second he thought about going inside, but he knew there wasn't time. Maybe after piano lessons, he thought. Clutching his music to his chest, he began to run the three blocks to Miss Talbot's house.

As he rounded the corner from Oakdale to Spring Street, he looked at his watch. 10:10. Yikes! His lesson was supposed to start at 10:00. How did it get so late? To make matters worse, he knew Miss Talbot would lecture him for not practicing. It was the same every Saturday. Each day he told himself he would practice later. But somehow the days went by, and then it was Saturday again and he hadn't practiced. His teacher at school, Mrs. Fogarty, said he had a problem with "time management." That was teacher talk for not getting his work done.

Breathing hard with each step, he saw Miss Talbot's white house. Good, almost there. He sprinted the last few feet to the gate and stopped to catch his breath. No sign of Angela anywhere, he thought, as he looked up the street. She's probably still inside. Just like her to stick around so she could rub it in that I'm late.

Angela Morgan was in Ryan's class at school. She also took piano lessons from Miss Talbot, and it was Ryan's bad luck that Angela had her lesson right before his. Angela was a goody-goody and a real pain. She loved to make fun of Ryan. Miss Talbot would say, "I hope you can play as well as Angela did." Then, when Miss Talbot turned her head, Angela would stick out her tongue.

The thought of Angela's face made Ryan frown. "I wish I didn't have stupid piano lessons," he said aloud.

"Saints be praised. 'Tis done," said a small voice.

"What?"

"I said, ' 'Tis done,' " said the voice. "Your wish is granted."

Ryan scratched his head and looked around. Nobody was there. A gust of wind swirled some dry leaves into a spiral. He looked up Spring Street. Kerry and Kurt Hunter, the six-year-old twins, were building a bike ramp on their driveway. He could hear them arguing over which board to use. Across the street, Mr. Mathews was digging in his flower bed. Ryan smelled the strong odor of fertilizer and wrinkled his nose.

"Over here," said the voice. "What do you use for eyes?"

Ryan turned around. His heart stopped for a second. On a low-hanging branch sat a strange-looking little man. He wore a green vest and pants and a green felt hat.

"What are you lookin' at?" the man asked as he crossed his arms across his chest.

Ryan blinked. Someone was playing a trick on him. It was probably one of Benji's friends in his St. Patrick's Day costume. But a creepy feeling inside told Ryan that the man was real.

The man appeared neat and tidy except for his feet. Each foot was wrapped in a bundle. Ryan guessed that at one time the bundles had been shoes. Made of pieces of leather, they were tied round and round with string.

The man pointed a long crooked finger at Ryan. "Saints be praised, I'm losin' me patience with you. Stop actin' like a toad."

Ryan stared at the man's wrinkled face. He wanted to run. But his legs wouldn't move. "Ahhh . . ." Ryan tried to talk, but no words came out.

"Rafferty," said the man, "you picked yourself a strange one. Can't speak a civil word."

"Uh . . . I can speak," Ryan said, finding his voice. "Who are you?"

"Rafferty McGill is the name." The man bounced off the branch to the ground, stood up, and removed his hat. With a sweep of his arm he bowed low, adding, "And who might you be?"

"Ryan. Ryan O'Conner. Are you a . . .?"

"A leprechaun, what else? From the first glorious moment of me birth."

"A leprechaun!" Ryan didn't want to believe his ears. "You can't be a leprechaun! Leprechauns aren't real."

"Not real, eh?" The man raised his voice. "NOT REAL? Leprechauns are as real as—" he paused and said, "you, standing there in pink pajamas."

"What?" Ryan looked down at his legs. "Oh, my gosh!" Sure enough, he was on Spring Street in pink pajamas with white bunnies on them. His shoes and clothes were gone. He wailed, "Oh, no!" His face turned red, and he shivered as the wind blew through the thin pajamas. Thunder sounded in the

distance. His bare feet were freezing. "Hey, get these off of me!"

Rafferty laughed. "Would you care for green?" Instantly the pajamas turned green. "Green, 'tis a grand color. Leprechauns love the color of green."

"Cut it out, mister!" Ryan shook with fear.

But the man continued. "How about the color of orange? That's a *real* color. Is purple real? How about goldenrod?" The pajamas changed colors as fast as Rafferty spoke the words. "Plaid? Turquoise?"

"OK! OK! You're real! Stop! Please!"

Immediately Ryan was back wearing his jeans and jacket. His legs felt wobbly as he sank down on a large rock next to the curb.

Rafferty laughed. "Och, now, Ryan, quite a dresser you are. Well, enough banterin'. Let's get down to business."

"Business?" Ryan's whole body felt like Jell-O. "What business?" he asked weakly.

"Why the wish-grantin' business," the man said sharply. "I granted your wish first, so now you'll be giving me mine." He smiled and rubbed his gnarly hands together. "I've been waiting a hundred years and a day. Me poor old feet have suffered so."

"Excuse me, sir," Ryan chose his words carefully, "but I don't know what you're talking about."

"Saints be praised! Rafferty McGill, you picked one worse than a cabbage. One without a brain." The man grumbled and began to pace back and forth. Suddenly he stopped in front of Ryan and shook his fist. "Look, you scalawag! Don't you know I removed your piano lessons?"

"What?" At the word *piano* Ryan looked at his watch. It was 10:20. "Oh, my gosh!" he moaned. "Miss Talbot is going to kill me!" He turned quickly and then stopped. Ryan was looking at a vacant lot. There was nothing there. He walked a few steps closer. There was no white frame house or porch.

"It's g . . . g . . . gone," Ryan whispered. "Miss Talbot's whole house is gone!"

# ✤ 2 ✤

# Vanished!

Of course, 'tis gone," said Rafferty. "You wished away your piano lessons."

"But Miss Talbot—" Ryan stared at the dirt where the house had stood.

"Who? What are you babbling about?"

"Miss Talbot . . . the lady who lives in the house, and her piano student, Angela." Ryan felt sick. "At least I think Angela was there."

Rafferty took off his cap and scratched his head. "Ummm. You say there was a lady and a young lass?"

"Yes!" Ryan shouted.

"Och, now, I am a bit rusty. Somehow they all got connected. I can't be bothered by details."

"But I didn't wish for *them* to be gone, just the piano lessons."

Rafferty shook his head. "Ah, just like a mortal, never satisfied." He gave Ryan a stern look and said,

"The facts be plain. Today is the end of me curse."

Ryan shook his head. "I don't understand."

Rafferty sighed and looked upward. "What a small brain you have. 'Tis very clear." He stared at Ryan and spoke slowly. "I've been wandering the underworld a hundred years and a day until this dratted curse was over. The king of the fairies himself placed the curse on me. I lost track of time and place, which is understandable, considering me situation. Suddenly, without any warning, the wandering is over. Pop! Here I am before your very eyes." Rafferty threw back his shoulders and placed his hands on his hips. "By command of the curse," he continued, "I'm to grant a wish to the first mortal I see. Then, in turn, the mortal is to grant me mine. I did me part." Rafferty brought his face close to Ryan's and raised his voice. "Now you grant me wish!"

Ryan's heart thumped loudly. "You've got to bring them back," he pleaded.

"Bring 'em back?" Rafferty spoke sharply. "I'll not be working any more wishes for you until I gets me own wish granted. Now hurry up. You've wasted enough time." Rafferty stood up straight and cleared his throat. In a loud voice he said, "I wish for a new pair of shoes."

Ryan's head hurt. This had to be a bad dream. "I can't grant wishes. I'm not magic. I'm just a boy."

"A boy!" Rafferty shrieked. "Boys are the worst kind of mortals!" With a rush of words, he continued, "I noticed you were a mite small but . . ." He paced back and forth. "You being the first mortal I laid me eyes on, I was desperate." He began to jump up and down, shouting, "The curse continues!" He shook his fist at the air. "Have you no mercy?" As if in answer, thunder rumbled across the sky.

Ryan watched Rafferty's jumping and shouting, all the while feeling more confused. Rafferty was acting just like his brother Benji did when Ryan beat him at a game of cards. But this wasn't a game. This was something serious. In a shaky voice he asked, "What are you shouting about?"

"'Tis bitter to have me tools taken from me, ill luck enough, but now to have to deal with a boy . . ." Rafferty threw himself down on the ground and pounded the grass with his fists. "King Tiranok, you've gone too far! No leprechaun should suffer me fate!"

Ryan didn't know what to do. He looked from the bare lot to the leprechaun and then back at the lot. Then he heard Kerry and Kurt yelling from up the street. "Hey, Mom," the twins yelled. "Look, look,

Miss Talbot's house is gone! Somebody took it!"

Mr. Mathews turned around from his gardening. His face turned white. He dropped his shovel. "Martha!" he shouted to his wife. "Call the police! Call 911!"

Mrs. Hunter came out of her house. At the sight of the vacant lot, her mouth dropped open. She and the twins hurried down the street and stood next to Ryan.

Mr. Mathews joined them, staring at the vacant lot.

"Wow!" said Kurt.

Kerry jabbed Ryan with his elbow. "Pretty cool, huh?"

Mrs. Hunter turned to the twins. "Boys, get home. Fast!"

"But Mom . . ."

"You heard me. Right now. Something strange is happening." She pushed both boys towards their house.

Ryan turned around to see if Rafferty was still there, but the leprechaun had disappeared. A police siren wailed a few blocks away. As it came closer, neighbors came out from their houses. Along with the siren, Ryan heard someone moaning. The sound came from an overgrown azalea bush a few feet away.

Ryan got on his knees and looked closer. Rafferty sat in the middle of the bush. "No, no," Rafferty moaned. "The banshee is wailing me death." He held his head in his hands. "Oh ohhhhhhh ohhhhhhh. Do you hear it, Ryan? Listen to her. It's the banshee. She's coming closer and closer to tell me me life is over. I'm doomed. Why, Rafferty McGill? Why did you have to choose a boy?" Rafferty moaned louder and louder. "Ohooooo ooooo oooooooo."

"Rafferty," Ryan said, "I don't know what a banshee is, but that's a police siren."

Rafferty didn't answer. Instead, his moans and the siren were joined by the wail of Mrs. Morgan. She ran towards them crying, "Angela! Angela! Where's my little girl?"

Ryan shuddered. Cripes, he thought, Angela *was* in the house. He didn't like Angela, but he didn't want her disappearing, either. "Rafferty, we have to tell someone what happened. Angela's mother or the—" Ryan peered into the bush. Rafferty was gone again.

A voice from the tree above said, "Tell? *Tell?*"

Ryan looked up and saw Rafferty on a branch, dangling his legs. How did he get there?

"I'll not be telling any mortal about meself. 'Tis against the fairy law. I'd sooner give up me gold."

21

"Well, I'm telling!" Ryan said sharply. He had had enough of this bully leprechaun. He took a step but immediately fell to the ground. Rafferty was back in the azalea bush. He had stuck out his leg and tripped Ryan.

"Owww, that hurt." Ryan rubbed his right knee and glared at the leprechaun.

Rafferty poked a bony finger into Ryan's arm. "Ryan, what would you tell? Would you tell everyone that you wished away your piano lessons? Who would believe you?"

"They'll believe me," Ryan said, trying to make his voice sound confident.

"And if you do tell," Rafferty's eyes grew blacker and blacker as he brought his wrinkled face close to Ryan, "I'll disappear, and the house and two females will be gone forever."

Ryan fought back tears as he rubbed his arm where Rafferty had poked him. What was he going to do?

Mr. Mathews bent over him. "Ryan, are you all right?" Startled, Ryan turned and looked into Mr. Mathews's pudgy face. Mr. Mathews put his hand on Ryan's forehead. "I heard you talking to yourself." Mr. Mathews looked as worried as he sounded.

Ryan looked from Mr. Mathews to Rafferty.

Rafferty crawled out from the bush, made a face, and stuck out his tongue. Mr. Mathews didn't seem to notice. Then it hit Ryan. *Mr. Mathews couldn't see Rafferty.*

"Ryan? I'm talking to you."

"Oh, yeah, sorry, Mr. Mathews. I'm OK. I'm kind of in shock. My lesson was next."

"You'll feel better in a few minutes. There must be some explanation." Mr. Mathews didn't sound like he believed what he was saying as he walked away.

Ryan stood there trying to sort things out. Was he the only one who could see Rafferty? A dog's low growl rumbled behind him. Oh, no, Brutus! The big black-and-gray German shepherd lived next door to Miss Talbot. Secretly, Ryan was afraid of all dogs, but everyone he knew was scared of Brutus. He looked at the raised fur on the back of Brutus's neck. This was not a good sign. Brutus's growling grew louder, and he strained at his leash. Ryan felt prickles on the back of his own neck. And then, with a sinking feeling, he knew. Brutus wasn't growling at the sirens or the people. He was growling at Rafferty. He could *see* Rafferty!

Brutus's upper lip curled, showing his fangs. He grew more frantic with his growls and lunges. The leash was hooked to a metal pole next to the house.

Horrified, Ryan saw the pole bending.

"Rafferty, we have to get out of here. FAST!"

"I'm not going anywhere until you grant me wish."

"But—" Ryan's panic increased. "Brutus might—"

With a mighty surge, the huge dog threw all his weight against the leash. The pole bent, and the leash slipped off. His fangs bared and dripping with drool, Brutus lunged at the two of them.

## ❧ 3 ❧

# Cowboy Rafferty
# and Other Tricks

Ryan froze. He knew the picket fence would not stop Brutus. As a blur of teeth and fur came towards them, Rafferty jumped over the fence and onto the dog's back.

Brutus howled and ran in small circles, trying to dislodge Rafferty. It looked like a scene from a Western movie. Rafferty was a cowboy riding a bucking bronco. The more Brutus turned, the more tangled he became in the leash that was still fastened to his neck. Finally, exhausted, Brutus keeled over on the ground.

"Saints be praised!" yelled Rafferty, grinning from ear to ear. He slid off the dog's back.

Brutus's eyes had a wild, fearful look. He lay panting and whimpering, the leather leash wound tightly

around his legs and body.

Mr. Mathews scratched his bald head and stared at Brutus. He climbed over the picket fence and untangled the big German shepherd. "I don't understand what's happening," he muttered. He straightened the pole and slipped the other end of the leash back in place. Brutus slunk to the far corner of the yard with his tail between his legs. Ryan felt kind of sorry for the dumb dog even though Brutus was always scaring the beejeebers out of him.

Rafferty clapped his hands together. "Nothing like a good ride to clear me mind." He laughed gleefully. "Now get on with it, boy."

"Rafferty," Ryan said, "how come Brutus can see you and Mr. Mathews can't?"

Rafferty crossed his arms. "Animals and young mortals cause me the most problems. As mortals grow older, they decide what's real and not real. If they decide that something's not real, then it ceases to exist in their minds." Rafferty grunted and looked disgusted. "Just like mortals to think they know everything. Most mortals can't see me even if I stand in front of them." He chuckled. "What a pitiful race humans are."

Rafferty walked over to the rock and sat down, one bony leg crossed over the other. "Once in a while an older mortal has a sense of belief. Then they are dangerous." His eyes became darker and his voice harsh. "Always poking around trying to catch a leprechaun or find the pot of gold at the end of the rainbow."

A white van screeched up to the curb. The letters WNEW were painted on the side. Four men piled out holding TV cameras and microphones. They shouted directions at one another. Then a pretty, dark-haired woman stepped out. Ryan recognized her immediately—Kit Summers from the five o'clock news. The men began setting up lights and cameras. To add to the commotion, a low whirring sound grew louder. Ryan looked up and saw a police helicopter approaching.

"What a strange place I've come to," Rafferty muttered softly, peering out from behind the rock. "And look at all them shoes."

A crowd gathered. People from up and down the street came to watch the TV crew and look at the ground where Miss Talbot's house had stood. The Hunter twins came back outside. Evidently Mrs. Hunter thought it was safe with so many police around. The twins headed straight for the cameraman. "Take my picture." "No, take mine." Kurt stuck his tongue out. With thumbs in his ears, Kerry wiggled his fingers and jumped up and down. "How about this?"

A man holding a microphone shouted over the sound of the helicopter that was circling Miss Talbot's vacant yard. "Kit Summers wants to talk to anyone who saw what happened. Are there any eyewitnesses?"

Ryan felt sick to his stomach.

Mr. Mathews and Mrs. Morgan crowded around the microphone. Mrs. Morgan was still crying. One of the cameramen thrust a camera close to her face. Ryan was so engrossed in watching the TV crew that he forgot about Rafferty.

"Break it up, folks." A policeman pushed his way through the crowd and into the circle around Kit Summers. And then, Ryan saw Rafferty on the ground next to the policeman. What was he doing?

The policeman said, "Everyone stay calm. There's a logical explanation." He took a step forward and fell to the ground. "Hey, what's—?"

Now the cameraman next to Mrs. Morgan went down, camera and all. "Who tied my shoelaces together?" he yelled. Ryan watched as one by one, each person wearing laced shoes tumbled to the ground, the shoelaces tied in knots.

"Rafferty, stop that!" Ryan yelled. Rafferty moved

from one person to another. No one seemed to see him. As soon as someone got his or her shoes untied, Rafferty tied them up again. Kit Summers, wearing high heels, ran back and forth between her crew members.

Kurt Hunter yelled, "Hey, look everybody! That little man is doing it. Catch him!" The twins dove into a pile of people. Oh, no! Ryan thought. The twins can see Rafferty, too! Kerry lunged for Rafferty. But the leprechaun was too quick. He popped out of reach and began tying the cords and cables from the microphones together. Kurt grabbed for him. Mrs. Hunter shouted, "Kurt, Kerry, stop it NOW!"

"But Mom, the man—"

Everyone was shouting and yelling. Ryan had to get Rafferty away before someone got hurt. He dropped to his hands and knees and crawled under a camera. Rafferty sat cross-legged, tying a knot in a microphone cord. "Stop it, Rafferty!"

Ryan grabbed Rafferty's arm and held it tightly. The arm was bony, with a sharp elbow. It felt more like a stick than an arm.

Rafferty looked up from his knot. "Saints be praised, Ryan, what a fine lad you are." He smiled, but the black eyes told Ryan that Rafferty was making fun of him.

"Save the talk, Rafferty. Just follow me."

"Follow you?"

"Yes. If you come home with me, I'll figure this out."

"Home with you?" For a second Rafferty stared at Ryan as if he were trying to read his mind. Then he smiled and said, "The boy has had a change of heart. Oh, 'tis my lucky day. My wish he'll be a-grantin'." Rafferty dropped the cords and wires.

Ryan shrugged. He didn't know about any wish-granting, but he did know that he had to get Rafferty out of there. Ryan gripped Rafferty's arm tightly, even though he knew he couldn't keep Rafferty from popping up somewhere else any time he wanted to. They walked down Spring Street. Ryan could still hear the confusion behind him. He glanced over his shoulder. Another police car had arrived. People still yelled at one another, but the cameras appeared to be working. Adding to the noise was Brutus's barking. Brutus was back to normal.

Rafferty began to skip and sing at the top of his voice. "Oh, 'tis my lucky day. The curse is gone far away." Ryan groaned.

Ryan's house was on Maple Avenue, which was the block behind Spring Street. His backyard neighbor was Mr. Gleason. Ryan planned to take a short-cut through the Gleasons' yard to his house. They had reached the bushes bordering the Gleasons' driveway when he heard one of the twins yell, "Hey, everybody, look! There's that weird little man. He's following Ryan!"

Ryan winced. He hadn't figured the twins would follow him.

Ryan dragged Rafferty along as he bolted to the backyard. Reaching the fence, Ryan grabbed hold of the top bar, hoisted himself up, and swung his legs over, landing in his yard.

Rafferty stood on the other side scratching his chin. "What exactly do you want me to do? You're behavin' like a rabbit."

"Rafferty, climb over the fence. Grab my hand and I'll help you."

"You're a regular tyrant with your orders. I do not climb."

Ryan ignored Rafferty's rudeness and held out his hand. Rafferty looked at Ryan with a sly grin and then disappeared! Ryan blinked. Immediately Rafferty reappeared, standing next to Ryan.

Ryan shook his head. He couldn't get used to the fact that Rafferty didn't do anything the way Ryan thought he should.

"Ryan! Ryan!" His mother called. "Where are you?"

Ryan turned around with alarm. Would his mom be able to see Rafferty? She might be one of those mortals Rafferty said could see him. She was pretty smart.

He had to hide the leprechaun.

# ❧ 4 ❧

# Poor Benji

Quick, Rafferty, hide!"

"Hide? I've had enough of your shenanigans. Now grant me wish!"

"Rafferty, if my mother catches you here, there'll be no time for wishes." Ryan searched his yard frantically. Where could he hide Rafferty? He looked at his tree house. "Quick, get up in my tree house!"

"Ryan!" His mother's voice sounded close to tears.

"Hurry, Rafferty," Ryan pleaded.

Rafferty stood stubbornly with his arms crossed.

Ryan's heart thumped wildly. "Please, Rafferty. I promise as soon as she's gone we'll talk about your wish."

"Saints be praised, now we're getting somewhere. Where is this tree house?"

Ryan pointed, and Rafferty disappeared, just as Ryan's mother came out on the back porch.

"Oh, Ryan." She rushed over to him, the worry on her face melting as she hugged him. "Didn't you hear me? I've been so scared. Something terrible has happened to Miss Talbot and Angela. I was afraid you were gone, too."

Ryan didn't know what to say.

His mother held him out at arm's length and gave him a hard look. "If you weren't at your piano lessons, where were you?"

"I was going . . . I was right there. In fact I was right by the gate when—"

"Then you saw it happen." His mother looked ready to cry. "They've vanished," she whispered. "Oh, I'm so glad you weren't in that house. This is all so terrible. Everyone in town is scared to death. They called off the St. Patrick's Day parade." She gave him another hug.

Ryan looked over his mom's shoulder as she hugged him, and there was Rafferty in full view, standing next to the tree house ladder.

Ryan squealed.

"Ryan, are you all right?" His mother stared at him. "Come into the house. I have to call your grandmother." She held his arm tightly.

"Mom, can I stay out here?" He eyed Rafferty nervously. Rafferty was jumping up and down, making faces, and waving his arms.

"Ryan, with the scare I've just had, I don't want you out of my sight."

"Mom, I'll stay right here in the yard. I'll stay . . . uh . . . in my tree house."

"No, Ryan, I don't like leaving you outside. I want you in the house or in the garage where I can find you." She thought for a moment and then said quickly, "You can sweep the garage like you're supposed to do."

"Mom, I'll sweep it later. Honest, I won't forget."

"Ryan you've said that three times this week."

"Mom, I really mean it. I'll only be in my tree house for a little while. Uh . . . to get over what happened to Miss Talbot." He put on his pleading face.

Ryan looked toward Rafferty who was standing on his head with his legs bent and his toes touching together. Sweat broke out on Ryan's forehead.

"Ryan, are you sure you're all right? You look a little pale." Mrs. O'Conner felt Ryan's forehead and then patted down the stray piece of hair that always stuck out by his ear.

The phone rang inside the house. His mother looked from the house to Ryan. "That's probably Grandma Betty. Oh, all right. You can stay out here, but don't leave this yard. And zip up your jacket.

And come in immediately if it starts to rain."

Ryan watched until she was inside before he turned back to his tree house. Thank goodness his mother hadn't seen Rafferty. Now the backyard was empty. Where did that leprechaun go, anyway? The only sound was the wind blowing through the pine trees that grew in the side yard.

Ryan climbed the ladder into the tree house. Rafferty was stretched out in one corner. "Whew!" Ryan sighed. He looked around the room. He hadn't been up here since last fall. The place needed a good sweeping. The floorboards were covered with dust, and the wind had blown dried leaves through the window. Along one wall were some old couch pillows his mom had given him and a blanket heaped in a mound. Under the window was a small shelf Ryan had made from some pieces of scrap wood.

Rafferty's feet were on a pillow, and the green hat was tilted down over his eyes. Ryan heard snoring followed by a wheezing, fluttering sound. But he knew Rafferty wasn't asleep. Just another trick!

"Wake up, Rafferty." He kicked the pillow out from under the ragged bundles that covered the leprechaun's feet.

"Ooooo," Rafferty sat up and rubbed his left ankle. "I've suffered so." Then his face brightened. "But me suffering is coming to an end because of Ryan. Ah, a grand and glorious name if ever there was one. Now down to business. A pair of shoes just right, to keep out the water and mud. And I wouldn't mind if they are grand to look at." He clasped his knees and rocked back and forth, filled with anticipation.

"Uh, Rafferty . . ." Ryan wasn't quite sure how to begin. Rafferty seemed to think that he, a mortal boy, had some power and could grant wishes. "Tell me what this is all about. I mean this curse stuff." Ryan figured if he stalled for time, he might get an idea. "Who put a curse on you?"

Rafferty eyed Ryan carefully. "You wouldn't be tricking me, boy, would you? Buttering me up, so you can steal me gold?"

"No, no. I just thought I'd be able to grant a better wish if I knew all the facts," Ryan said, trying to sound nonchalant.

"Well, I guess it won't hurt . . . a few more minutes after all these years." Rafferty stood up. He lowered his voice. "But I'll not be telling any mortal about me gold. 'Tis against the fairy law. And . . ." Rafferty came so close that Ryan could hardly keep his balance.

The leprechaun's face darkened, and his eyes narrowed to black slits. He poked a finger into Ryan's chest as he said slowly, "I'll . . . not . . . be . . . tricked . . . out of it."

"OK, OK," Ryan said, backing away. "I won't ask about your gold. Don't get so touchy."

Rafferty went back to the corner, propped his feet up again on the pillow, and began his story.

"I'm a cobbler, and the best in all the Emerald Isle."

"Cobbler? What's that?"

"Why, a shoemaker, of course. Is your head filled with sawdust? Who else other than cobblers makes shoes?"

"Mine came from—oh, never mind." Ryan decided that there was no point in telling Rafferty about Super Shoe City where his mom bought his shoes.

"Ryan, Ryan," Benji's high-pitched whine interrupted them.

Ryan stuck his head out the window. "What do you want?"

"Can I come up?" Benji was still dressed in his leprechaun costume.

"No, go away."

"Ryan, you're mean. I'm coming up anyway. You can't stop me. I'll tell Mom."

"Stay out, Benji!" Ryan yelled. But Benji began to climb the ladder. Oh, no! The last thing Ryan needed was Benji up in the tree house with Rafferty.

"Ryan," Rafferty said, "who and what is that green creature interrupting me story?"

"That's my brother, and he's not green. He's supposed to be a leprechaun. Whoops—I mean—" Ryan stopped, somehow knowing Rafferty would not approve.

"What! A leprechaun?"

"For the St. Patrick's Day parade, Rafferty. Lots of little kids are dressed like leprechauns."

Rafferty looked as if someone had thrown a bucket of ice water on his head. Then he shook his fist at the ceiling and shouted, "King Tiranok, how much humiliation must me poor soul endure? And in the name of St. Paddy himself. You're a cruel one, Tiranok!"

Outside, Benji slowly climbed each rung, chanting, "I'm coming up and you can't stop me. I'm coming up and you can't—"

"Benji," Ryan yelled, "stay down, *please*." Then Ryan saw Rafferty on the ground below. "Quick, Benji, get down!" But it was too late. Ryan smelled a horrible strong odor of rotting garbage. Suddenly green slime poured down from the tree house.

The rungs of the ladder were covered.

Benji lost his footing and fell to the ground. He started crying. The green slime oozed over him. His hands and face were covered with it. "I'm telling. I'm telling on you, Ryan!"

Ryan watched Benji go in the back door. Poor Benji, he thought. He's no match for Rafferty's tricks. Ryan heard Rafferty chuckling down below. He said sharply, "Rafferty, that was a mean thing to do. That green stuff is horrible!" Ryan held his nose. "Phew!" The smell made his eyes water.

Rafferty nodded. "Ah, yes, thank you kindly for noticing." He laughed again.

Ryan's face flushed with anger. "But Benji's only a little kid," he sputtered.

"Size is of no matter, Ryan. 'Tis the fairy law that only leprechauns may dress as leprechauns."

Ryan didn't know anything about fairy law but he did know that dealing with Rafferty was worse than dealing with anyone he'd ever known, even Angela! In an angry voice he ordered, "Rafferty get back up here!"

Rafferty chuckled. "Tsk, tsk, what a temper you have, lad." And then he was gone.

# King Tiranok and the Curse

Ryan turned around and Rafferty was back in the corner of the tree house. The green slime odor was still in the air. "Yuck!" Ryan said, keeping his nose pinched so he didn't breathe in more of it. Rafferty cleared his throat and began again. "As I was about to say, I was hired by the king of the fairies, King Tiranok himself, to mend the shoes of the fairy folk. There was a huge fairy fort near me tree." Rafferty paused and his eyes grew misty. "Ah, me thorn tree. The best possible home."

"You lived in a tree?"

"Of course not! Anyone with a brain knows that leprechauns live underground, comfortably among the roots." He stopped and looked around. "However, Ryan, I must tell you that this tree house of yours is not bad. You do have more of a view." He stretched his arms over his head and yawned. "But of course it's not hidden and would be easily seen by mortals."

"Rafferty," Ryan said impatiently, "get on with your story." He grabbed the old blanket and spread it on the floor so he could sit.

"Where was I?" Rafferty asked. "Yes. King Tiranok and his fairies brought me more and more pairs of boots and shoes to mend. Such a heap of work, I thought I'd best rest up and get some sleep. I told meself I'd get to the shoes first thing in the morn. But then the next day dawned like a bright new jewel. Such a grand and glorious sky. Sure, I could not stay cooped up in me home. How could a body work with the sun shining on the hills?" Rafferty stood up. "The facts be plain, I fully intended to get to me labors. Och sure, but before I could blink, a week and a day slipped by."

Rafferty's words made Ryan feel a little uneasy. He thought of his teacher, Mrs. Fogarty, when he turned his homework in late.

Rafferty continued. "Then, just as I sat down at me bench, King Tiranok knocks at me door and asks for the shoes." Rafferty's eyes burned like two coals and his face flushed. "I told him I took a little rest but I'd be done by the morn. Sure, I meant no harm and

I thought he would be understandin'. But instead he boils up like a cauldron and screams a curse. 'A rest you want, then a rest you shall have! You shall wander the underworld for a hundred years and a day *without* your tools.' "

Rafferty stopped for a moment, too overcome with emotion to continue. He shrugged his shoulders. "So I could not mend me shoes or make meself another pair." He lowered his voice. "Which is, as anybody knows, against the fairy law. Leprechauns mend their shoes as soon as they show a bit of wear."

Rafferty sat down, looking tired. He pulled up his right foot and tightened the twine holding the leather scraps in place. "Ah, why I didn't just mend the shoes and be over with it?" He sighed deeply.

"Well, that explains your feet," Ryan said. "I wondered how they got like that."

"And to make matters worse, old Tiranok gives all his shoes that need mending to me worst enemy, Patrick O'Shaunessey. Such a scoundrel that Patrick is! For all these years he's been rubbing it in and telling everyone that'll listen about me fate." Rafferty imitated Patrick with a high-pitched, sing-song voice, " 'Rafferty McGill, the worst cobbler in the Emerald Isle.' Och, sure, the pain I've endured."

Ryan thought, just like Angela's teasing. He

understood how Rafferty felt.

The leprechaun's voice sounded thin and tired. "At the end of a hundred years and a day, I'm to grant a wish to the first mortal that I see. Then that mortal in turn grants mine. Once that happens, I've fulfilled the requirements of Tiranok's curse and me tools are given back to me."

Rafferty raised his voice. "Since I can't make meself a pair of shoes until I have me tools, I am forced to wish for a new pair." He paused. "And as sure as I am Rafferty McGill, today when I popped up from the underworld, you were the first mortal me poor eyes saw. And as luck would have it, immediately you made a wish, and I granted it. There, you have me story. So get on with it. Me patience is finished. Grant me wish quickly!"

Ryan was quiet. He stared out the window for a few seconds and then said, "I'm sorry for what happened to you. I think that king is real mean, and so is that other cobbler." He paused, searching for the right words. "You still have ill luck, because when I told you that I couldn't grant wishes, it was the truth. King Tiranok must have known that mortals can't grant wishes, at least not the ones I know."

Ryan covered his ears and closed his eyes, expecting an explosion of temper from Rafferty. But everything was still. He opened his eyes and looked at Rafferty. A large tear trickled slowly down the wrinkled old face. Did leprechauns cry? Or was this another trick?

"I'm sorry, Rafferty," Ryan said weakly. The only sounds were the rubbing noises the branches made against the tree house each time the wind blew.

After a few seconds, Rafferty muffled a sob. "Me fate is sealed," he said sadly. "Our proud family line has come to this. Never shall I see me home."

Puzzled, Ryan asked, "Why won't you see your home again?"

"It would be a disgrace to return. Och, I could not bear to have that good-for-nothing Patrick shouting me misfortune to every passerby. And I can't go home with these bundles of twine. I'd be the joke of the Emerald Isle. Who would give a cobbler work when he doesn't have tools or a pair of shoes?" He lowered his voice to a whisper. "After all this time, King Tiranok, you've won." Rafferty took out a huge red handkerchief and blew his nose with a loud honk.

Ryan felt sorry for him. He tried to think of what he could do to help. He could go to Super Shoe City, but he didn't have any money. And there was no way he could ask his parents for money without telling them about Rafferty. Ryan looked at his own shoes. They were much too big for the leprechaun.

Suddenly Rafferty stood up. "Well, saints be praised, if this is to be me new home, I'll make the best of it. Never have it be said that Rafferty McGill is a poor loser." He walked around the room. "Let's see. I can use that shelf for me bench, for old time's sake. And I'll need more pillows here and—"

"Wait a minute," Ryan interrupted. "What are you doing?"

"Why, I'm plannin' me new home. I can't go back with me feet like this, so I'll be comfortable here."

"But you can't—this is my—" The words wouldn't come out. His tree house was his own special hideaway. He wasn't going to share it with anyone, least of all a bossy leprechaun. He found his voice. "You can't stay here!" he shouted.

Rafferty gave him a sly smile. " 'Tis your fault that I can't go back."

"*My* fault?" Ryan couldn't believe what he was hearing. "I didn't put the curse on you. I had nothing to do with any of this."

"Stop whining like a piglet. It's time for me dinner. Baked soda bread and some good Irish ale." Rafferty rubbed his hands together. "This may work out after all, me living with mortals."

"But I'll tell everybody about you," Ryan said, feeling helpless.

Rafferty broke into a cackling laugh. "Tell anybody you wish."

"But you said you'd leave if I told anyone."

"So I did, so I did. But I also said I'd not be bringing back your Miss Talbot and Angela. Believe what you will, Ryan, but get me dinner. And be quick about it."

Ryan climbed down the rungs of the ladder, his insides ready to explode. Miss Talbot and Angela were missing. Everyone in town was scared. Benji had been treated horribly, and now his own special tree house was being taken from him. Things were going from bad to worse. How was he going to get Miss Talbot and Angela back?

Time was running out.

# ✿ 6 ✿

# Big Trouble

**R**yan slammed the back door. Who did Rafferty think he was? Giving him orders. Telling him to get baked soda bread and ale. What the heck was soda bread, anyway? Well, Ryan would show him. He'd make him wait until he was good and hungry. And then it would be peanut butter and jelly. Take it or leave it.

Ryan's mother walked into the kitchen. "Ryan, where did you get that horrible, smelly stuff that you threw on Benji?" She crossed her arms and tapped her foot.

"Mom, I didn't—"

"Ryan, don't lie to me. How could you pick on your brother at a time like this?"

Ryan's face grew hot. "But Mom—"

She interrupted him. "You know how upset

everyone is. Go tell Benji you're sorry right this minute." She turned and walked angrily out of the room.

Darn that Rafferty! Ryan went into the family room. Benji was on the couch, still wearing his leprechaun hat. The rest of his costume was probably in the washing machine. A superhero cartoon was on the TV. Benji looked up at Ryan and said, "You're the meanest brother in the whole world." He stuck out his lower lip in a pout.

"Benji, I'm sorry about what happened. I told you not to come up the ladder."

"You didn't have to put that green yucky stuff all over me." He sniffed a big sniff.

"Honest, Benji, I'm sorry. I'll make it up to you as soon as I work something out."

Ryan flopped on the sofa and looked at the cartoons. But his mind kept going over Miss Talbot's and Angela Morgan's disappearance. What if they never came back?

Why had he made that stupid wish? Piano lessons weren't *that* bad. And if he practiced . . .

Ryan went over to the piano in the living room. His fingers lightly touched the white keys. He liked the feel of the hard, slick surfaces. Sitting down on the bench, he played each of his songs slowly. Then he played them again.

Ryan knew that he really *liked* playing piano. For a few minutes he sat there thinking quietly, staring at the notes of his music. I'm just like Rafferty, he said to himself, always putting things off until later. He clenched his fists and made up his mind. When Miss Talbot came back, he was going to do things differently. He would show her and Mrs. Fogarty. And then the full weight of what had happened hit. What if Miss Talbot never came back? And Angela? Ryan felt a blackness come over him, as if he had fallen down a deep, dark hole.

"We interrupt this program to bring you an update from our newsroom about mysterious happenings on Spring Street." Ryan's stomach lurched. He walked back to the family room where Kit Summers's face looked out from the TV screen. "We have several strange things to report on this St. Patrick's Day. We are on the scene at 5735 Spring Street.

"At exactly 10:10 this morning, a house belonging to Margaret Talbot disappeared. Miss Talbot and one of her piano students, Angela Morgan, were in the house at the time of the disappearance. Investigators are still looking for clues." The screen showed the vacant lot surrounded by yellow plastic tape and "Do Not Enter" signs. Several men with instruments and small boxes that looked like metal detectors moved across the dirt.

Ryan's mother came into the room and stood behind him. "Oh, this is dreadful," she said.

Kit Summers continued. "Neighbors report other mysterious events involving a dog. I myself witnessed unexplained knots in our cable and microphone equipment. Authorities want to talk to anyone with any information. Several children on the street reported seeing an odd little man. No one knows if this man is involved. I have with me Kerry and Kurt Hunter."

Kit Summers held the microphone out to her left. And right there on TV were the Hunter twins. Benji pointed. "Hey, Ryan, look!"

Ryan didn't have to be told to look. His eyes bugged out as the twins made faces into the camera. Then Kerry said, "We saw this weird little man. He was tying everybody's shoes together with their strings. We tried to catch him."

"Yeah," Kurt continued. "But then the man went down the street with Ryan O'Conner."

"Yeah," Kerry interrupted, "we saw him with Ryan."

Ryan felt like he was going to throw up his

breakfast.

Benji shouted, "Ryan, they said your name! You're on TV!"

The Hunter twins started making faces into the camera again. Kit Summers moved the microphone away. "The police are following all leads, and we hope to have some information soon. Now returning to our studio, this is Kit Summers from WNEW."

The screen went to a toothpaste commercial and then back to the cartoon. Ryan's mother stared at the screen with her mouth open.

"That . . . that was *you* the boys were talking about," his mother said slowly. "Ryan, what did they mean? What little man?" She looked over her shoulder. "There isn't anything or . . . anyone in the house, is there?"

Ryan's hands felt cold and clammy. What should he say? He wanted to tell his mother all about Rafferty and the piano lessons. But she'd never believe him.

"Ryan?"

Ryan shuffled his feet and put his hands in his pockets. The jarring ring of the doorbell startled both of them.

"What now?" his mother muttered as she went to answer it. She returned immediately, the color drained from her face. "There are reporters and TV people out there. They want to talk to you. They think you know something about what's happened."

Ryan tried to speak, but his throat felt like a baseball was blocking it.

# Peanut Butter and Give-Away Clothes

The phone rang.

"Don't answer it," his mother said sharply.

"But, Mom, what if it's Dad or Grandma?"

"Ryan, do as I say. Lock the back door and pull all the drapes and shades. You're not talking to anyone until your father gets home. And then you're going to tell us everything you know about this." Ryan knew better than to argue with her. He nodded silently. She gave him a strange, sideways look.

Ryan went from window to window, pulling the drapes. From the dining room he could see the front yard. Strangers were standing and pointing at his house. As he stepped in front of the window, they saw him. A shout went up from the crowd. "There he is! That's Ryan!"

Quickly he closed the drapes. He took a big breath, trying to calm his racing heart. That darn Rafferty was ruining his life!

To reach the laundry room window, Ryan had to move a large bag of give-away clothes. Last week his mother had cleaned out the closet in his and Benji's room. As he pulled the shade, he noticed the toe of Benji's pink high-top tennis shoe sticking out of the bag.

Ryan stopped and then slowly pulled the shoes out of the bag. "Sure," he said out loud. "Why not, these should fit. Why didn't I think of this before? Rafferty needs shoes. Just give him some shoes!"

Ryan raced to the kitchen. He took out the peanut butter and jelly jars and two slices of bread. If Rafferty had food, he might be more agreeable to wearing Benji's shoes. As he slathered peanut butter on the bread, he wished Benji had chosen a shoe color other than pink. Green would have been perfect. But pink or no pink, they were all Ryan had.

The sandwich made, he grabbed his thermos and filled it with water. Then, slowly, he opened the back door. A light rain had started to fall. Ryan looked around, but no one was watching. Everyone seemed to be out in the front yard. He bolted across the back yard to the tree house ladder.

Ryan placed his foot on the lowest rung and shoved the tennis shoes under his left arm. It was hard to climb the wet ladder with the shoes, thermos, and sandwich. Thank goodness the slime was gone. He stuffed the thermos into the top of his pants and held the sandwich in his mouth.

Then he heard, "Hey, there's Ryan! We told you he'd go to his tree house!" Ryan turned his head. The Hunter twins, dressed in yellow rain slickers, stood in Mr. Gleason's backyard.

"Hey, Ryan!" they called, together. A policeman stood next to the boys, holding Brutus on a leash. Brutus barked furiously and lunged at the Gleasons' fence. Several men with metal detectors were also in the yard. Ryan ignored the twins as he scrambled up the ladder.

The trap door was shut. Ryan banged the top of his head against the wooden board. Brutus's barking grew louder. The policeman yelled something, but Ryan couldn't make it out with all the noise. Rain was falling harder. Ryan's tee shirt was wet and clingy. Why hadn't he put on his jacket?

Open, Rafferty, open, he thought. He tried to yell, but the sandwich garbled his words. Frantically he banged the top of his head again on the trap door. This time Rafferty opened the door a crack and said, "You wouldn't be me arch-enemy Patrick O'Shaunessy, would you?"

Ryan shook his head, almost losing the sandwich.

"Would you be a mortal?"

Ryan nodded.

"Well, no mortals allowed." Rafferty chuckled and closed the door. Ryan thought he would explode. This was no time for Rafferty to be playing games.

"OKKked thh drrr!" He tried to speak.

Rafferty opened the door again, just a crack. Out of the corner of his eye, Ryan could see the twins climbing over the fence. Another few seconds . . .

Then Rafferty spied the sandwich in Ryan's mouth. "I will make an exception for this mortal," he said in a loud voice. "He has brought me dinner. It will save me poor starving body." With that, Rafferty opened the trap door wider. Ryan popped up through the floor and slammed the door shut behind him.

# ✤ 8 ✤

# The Curse Is Far Away

Well, saints be praised, Ryan. I thought you'd left me here to starve to me death."

Rain dripped from Ryan's face. He took the sandwich and gave it to Rafferty. "I'm sorry it's a little soggy and there's a bite out of it. It was the only way I could carry it. And here's some water." He handed Rafferty the thermos.

A voice called up. "Hey, Ryan, come on out!" It was Kurt. "Or else let us come up." Ryan dropped to his knees and crawled to the window. He flattened himself against the side wall and peeked out. Kurt and Kerry were directly underneath the tree house. As far as he could tell they were the only ones in the yard. The others must have gone around to the front instead of climbing the Gleasons' fence. "Come on, Ryan. We're your friends. Let us up."

Ryan whispered so the boys couldn't hear him.

"Rafferty, there's not much time." He shivered in his wet tee shirt.

"What do you have under your arm, boy?" Rafferty asked as a slow smile crossed his face.

"Here, try these, Rafferty. They're shoes. Tennis shoes."

"Tennis shoes?" Rafferty took the pair from Ryan's hand and looked at them carefully, turning them over and over.

Ryan held his breath. He could hear Brutus barking below. A man's voice called up. "Ryan, come down. We'd like to talk to you."

Ryan ignored the voice. It seemed as if Rafferty was taking forever to examine the shoes.

"Never have I seen such shoes. What kind of leather is on the soles?"

"That's rubber, Rafferty. Better than leather. You can run and jump real high with rubber soles. Try them on. Hurry."

Again the man's voice called up. "Ryan, I'm with the police department. I want to ask you some questions. There's nothing to be afraid of."

Rafferty seemed unaware of the commotion below as he sat down on the bench and slowly unwound the twine holding the scraps of leather on his feet.

Ryan wanted to scream at Rafferty to hurry, but this was not the time to get him angry. Very carefully the leprechaun slipped on the pink high tops and laced them up. He stood up and took a few steps. He sat down and then stood and walked again.

"Well?" Ryan asked, not able to wait any longer. "Do they fit?"

Rafferty looked up at Ryan, and a broad grin broke across his wrinkled face. "Like a glove!" he shouted. "You did it, Ryan! You granted me wish. And they are the grandest I've ever seen!"

Rafferty took off his hat and bowed low as he had done when Ryan first met him. "Ryan, I've changed me mind about boys." And with that, Rafferty jumped in the air and snapped his heels together. Then he danced a jig, singing, " 'Tis my lucky day. The curse is far away!"

Ryan clapped his hands and smiled at the leprechaun's dancing.

"Ryan!" his father's voice interrupted them. "Ryan, are you up there? Come down right now!"

Ryan stuck his head out the window. Flashes of light blinded him for a second as photographers snapped his picture. He blinked and then shielded his eyes from the rain. "Hi, Dad. What's up?" He tried to sound normal.

"Ryan!" his father said sternly.

"Uh, sorry, Dad. I'll be right down." He pulled his head back in. Whew, thank goodness, Ryan thought. That was close. I fixed Rafferty's curse just in time!

Relief and joy made Ryan feel like dancing a jig with Rafferty and singing at the top of his lungs, "The curse is far away."

# ✦ 9 ✦

# A Wish in Time

Ryan turned around. "Quick, Rafferty, bring back Miss Talbot and Angela and Miss Talbot's house. I told my dad I'd be right down. Hurry!"

Rafferty sat down and put his right foot across his left knee. He rubbed a speck of dirt off the shoe with his elbow. "Ryan, we have a small problem."

"Problem!" Ryan shrieked. "What problem? Bring them back! You said you would. I did what you wanted. You have a pair of shoes."

"That I do. That I do. The problem is, I can only grant one wish. You are askin' for three. Which will it be . . . to bring back Miss Talbot or Miss Angela or the house? Choose away, and I'll be gone today."

"But you made them all disappear at the same time!"

The leprechaun scratched his chin and cocked his head to the side. "I'm still not quite sure how that happened. But I do know 'tis against the fairy law to grant more than one wish. So choose."

"How can I choose?" Ryan felt near tears.

"Ryan," Rafferty said, irritated, "the curse is gone. Don't keep me waiting. I'm anxious to get me thorn tree and me tools back. And I can't wait to see the look on old Patrick's face when he finds that Rafferty McGill is back and wearing the finest shoes in the land. So saints be praised, boy, make up your mind."

"But—but—"

His father's voice, now angry, interrupted again. "Ryan, I'm soaking wet. COME DOWN RIGHT NOW!"

Ryan forced his brain to think. There had to be a way. There *had* to be. "Rafferty, you can only grant me one wish, right?"

Rafferty sighed. "Yes, what a slow brain you have." He twisted his toes and admired the backs of the tennis shoes. "Never have I seen a color like this. What did you call it?"

"Pink! They're pink!" Ryan screamed, frantically trying to concentrate on how to fix this mess. "Only one wish, one wish," he repeated to himself.

Rafferty grew impatient. "Ryan, I won't be put off of me home any longer. Time's up. I'm—"

"Wait!" Ryan shouted. He had the answer! "OK," he said, "I wish the time was back to 10:09 exactly."

" 'Tis done!"

Ryan barely heard the words spoken, looked around, and there he was on Spring Street. He felt out of breath, as if he had just run from Oakdale to Spring Street. Clutched to his chest was his piano music.

"It worked! It worked!" he yelled.

He turned around and there was Miss Talbot's house, Miss Talbot's BEAUTIFUL house. Up the street the Hunter twins were building a bike ramp in their driveway. Across the street Mr. Mathews was digging in his garden. Even the fertilizer smelled wonderful.

"Everything is perfect!" Ryan shouted.

"You're in a good mood today," Mr. Mathews said, smiling at him.

Ryan turned and looked carefully at the low tree branch and the large rock near the curb. No sign of Rafferty. He must be back under his thorn tree. Ryan smiled, knowing that Rafferty was the only leprechaun in the Emerald Isle with pink high-top tennis shoes.

Ryan pushed open Miss Talbot's gate and with a high-pitched "Yahoo!" raced up the steps. The door opened and Miss Talbot said, "Good morning, Ryan. You're late again." Standing next to Miss Talbot was Angela with a smirk on her face.

Ryan was so glad to see both of them. He didn't even mind Angela's smirk. Words tumbled out of him. "Yes, Miss Talbot, I'm really sorry, honest. I won't be late anymore, and from now on I'm going to practice and I'm going to play as well as Angela."

And then, before Angela could wipe the surprised look off her face, Ryan said, "Saints be praised, Angela. Happy St. Patrick's Day!"

## ABOUT THE AUTHOR

Dianne MacMillan grew up in St. Louis, Missouri, and graduated from Miami University in Ohio with a degree in education. She taught elementary school for many years. For the past twenty-six years, she has devoted her time to writing books and stories for children. Among her titles are books about endangered animals, California history, and holidays. One of her favorite holidays is St. Patrick's Day.

As a child, Ms. MacMillan, who is part Irish, loved tap-dancing Irish jigs. Today she lives with her husband in Anaheim, California, and is still hoping to see a leprechaun.